AMAZING SHORT STORIES
FOR GROWN-UPS

AMAZING SHORT STORIES FOR GROWN-UPS

VOLUME 1

RICHARD DENNIS MAYS

Charleston, SC
www.PalmettoPublishing.com

Amazing Short Stories for Grown Ups
Copyright © 2020 by Richard Dennis Mays

Hardcover ISBN: 978-1-64990-486-7
Paperback ISBN: 1-64990-486-X

ACKNOWLEDGEMENTS

I would like to thank my mother and grandmother, who taught me work ethic, determination, and to never give up no matter what. I would like to thank my father, who taught me that it is never too late to make up for lost time; and my stepfather, for teaching me patience and that you don't always have to be loud to get your point across. I would also like to thank my kids and grandkids, who changed my entire life. You mean so much to me and I am so proud of you. To my brothers, sisters, aunts, uncles, nieces, nephews, cousins, and friends, I appreciate all the support and encouragement you all have given me over the years, I love you all so very much. I cannot express enough thanks to my Military and Veterans Affairs family for their continued love and support. For all the women in my life who have helped me become the man I am today, I am so grateful. You know who you are. I would like to thank all my teachers from grade school to high school, college, and the military.

TABLE OF CONTENTS

STORY NO. 1:

WRITTEN BY RICHARD DENNIS MAYS

AGE AIN'T NOTHING BUT A NUMBER

Lisa Jenkins was the owner of Sunshine Dry Cleaners. Her friend Beth and her daughter Fay ran the cleaner's day-to-day operations.

It was a bright sunny day and the street was busy. A man got out of his car and walked inside the store. Lisa's daughter, Fay, was inside, busy at the front counter. She looked up at the man as he approached her. He was in his early 40s and was of medium height. His name was Austin Johnson. As he reached

Fay, she asked with a gentle smile on her face, "Hello Sir, may I help you?"

Austin was very attracted by her lovely face. He also replied with a gentle smile.

"Yes, beautiful, I was driving by and saw your establishment. I need these few items dry cleaned as soon as possible. I don't care about the cost. You think you can help me?"

Fay nodded and said, "Sure, we can do that, we can have these done in a couple of hours. We are not that busy today."

Austin was taken by her wonderful way of speaking. He wasn't able to stop himself from giving her a compliment.

"I apologize, but you are breathtaking. I love the way you smile; you brighten up this whole place. You are the most beautiful woman I have ever met."

Fay felt shy. "I don't know about that, but thank you."

"I hate to be forward, but what are you doing tonight? I am having a party on my yacht this evening with a few friends. I was hoping you could join me?"

Lisa, who was noticing everything from the back room, finally came forward and jumped into their conversation.

"She has homework to do. She is a student at the university. Don't you think you are a little too old to be trying to take my 22-year-old daughter out, Sir? How old are you, anyway?"

Austin was a bit surprised by her reply. "My apologies, ma'am. My name is Austin Johnson, and I am 42 years old. I don't think my age should matter if it doesn't matter to your beautiful amazing daughter here, with all due respect."

Fay didn't like her mother's behavior. She said, "You don't have to apologize, Austin, I make my own decisions, and yes, I accept your invitation. What time do you want me to be there?"

Austin looked at her and smiled. "Here is my card; call me, and I will send a car for you. I promise, ma'am; I will take perfect care of your daughter, and you are invited as well. Have you ever been on a yacht? I'm sure you will enjoy it."

"No, thanks. And yes, I have been on a yacht."

Austin left after listening to her reply. Fay looked at Lisa, frustrated. "Mom, please stop trying to ruin my life! I will call you later."

Before Lisa could say anything, Fay left. A minute later, Beth arrived for her shift.

"Lisa, who was that fine man leaving in that pretty sports car?" asked Beth.

Lisa looked at her and replied, "Some old cradle robber!"

"Cradle robber?"

"Some old ass man was trying to talk to Fay, asking her out on his yacht, preying on young girls with his money. He asked me along too, but I told him I've been on plenty of yachts and didn't need to see his."

"He didn't look old to me. Wait a minute, he has a yacht? Jay Z and Beyoncé don't have a yacht. Lisa, when were you ever on a yacht?"

"Shut up, girl, you know I have never been on no yacht. I just didn't want him to think he was all that."

Shortly after, another customer entered the store. His name was Dexter Tate, and he was a student from the university. Lisa noticed him and said, "Can I help you, Sir?"

Dexter smiled, saying, "Yes ma'am, you may, I have some shirts that need dry cleaning."

Lisa nodded. "Sure, we can do that for you. I've never seen you around here before, are you new in town?"

Before he could reply, Beth jumped in between them. "No, we have never seen you around. We would've remembered your sexy ass. Damn, you're fine. I am a white girl who likes young dark meat."

Lisa felt a bit awkward. "Beth! Please excuse her, Sir; my friend is very outspoken."

"Well, if you want me to shut up, I will," said Beth.

Again Dexter smiled and replied, "No problem, and please stop calling me sir. I saw your sister leaving. I think she attends the university with me. I think we have a class together."

Lisa blushed. "That's not my sister. That's my daughter, and whatever you're selling, young man, I am not buying."

Dexter sighed. "My apologies, but I'm not selling anything. You look amazing, and your smile makes my heart soar. You must have amazing genes; you look so young for your age."

Beth was utterly lost in gazing at Dexter. Again she said, "Girl, I'm telling you, if you don't want him, I'll take him."

"We get it, Beth. Don't you have something in the back to do?"

Beth shook her head. "Okay. I will go in the back, but if you need me...."

"Where are you from, Dexter?"

"I was born in Jamaica and raised in Brooklyn. Most of my family are still in Jamaica. Tell me, Lisa. May I call you Lisa?" said Dexter.

"Yes, you may."

"You own this business?"

"Yes, I have two cleaners. I have another one on the west side of town as well."

"Brains and beauty all wrapped in one. When can I see more of you, Lisa?"

Lisa felt a bit surprised. "Dexter, I am twice your age, young man," she replied.

"Age shouldn't matter, only if you think so. Maybe we can have lunch tomorrow, yes?"

"Sure, I don't think anything would be wrong with lunch."

Dexter smiled and said, "Let me see your cell phone. Here's my number. Give me a call."

He typed his phone number in her phone, and then left.

Beth came to her with a smile on her face. Lisa was looking straight ahead, lost in thought.

"You go, girl. He is tall, dark, and handsome."

"He is perfect. And that accent," said Lisa.

Beth smiled. "Let me guess, makes you wet."

Lisa shook her head. "Beth, why is your mind always in the gutter," she said.

"But Lisa, I thought you had a problem with age. You don't want to rob that cradle!"

Lisa looked confused. "What do you mean?"

"You hit the roof when that guy asked Fay out, that sounds to me like a double standard."

"That's different. Fay is my baby. Plus, older men only date younger women because of physical attraction or money."

"So, you don't like Dexter because of your physical attraction to him?" asked Beth.

"No, I like his maturity for his age. Plus, I would be judged more harshly than he would anyway because I would be an older woman dating a younger man."

Beth was trying to change her mentality, but Lisa had a reply to everything. Again she tried. "Whatever! You don't think Fay is mature? You raised her right, Lisa. She is responsible and can take care of herself."

Lisa felt those words and realized her mistakes. "You are right, girl."

Beth smiled, knowing that she had been successful in what she was trying to do. "Yeah, girl."

"That's why I love you."

They smiled, looking at each other. Lisa had changed her opinion. Beth knew it. Lisa's mentality towards the difference between the ages was now fully cleared up. And that's what is called a perfect ending.

THE END

WRITTEN BY RICHARD DENNIS MAYS

AMORE

Rosa Bell Singleton was a young Black female house-keeper living with her employers, a wealthy white couple, Thomas and Beth Rogers. Thomas Rogers was the owner and CEO of Cee & Cee Cosmetics, one of the top cosmetics companies in the United States. Rosa had become pregnant by her estranged boyfriend and had twin girls. Rosa told the Rogerses that her boyfriend left her and moved back to Italy. Thomas and Beth did not mind having the kids around. Beth was never able to have children, so they were very fond of Rosa's twin daughters, Amore and Bella. The two girls were not identical twins. In fact, Amore was very light-skinned, and Bella was dark; but both were very beautiful, smart, and energetic.

One day, Rosa was walking down the street, very close to the Rogers' house. Another woman looked at Rosa as she approached. She said, with a smile on her face, "Hello Rosa, where is that pretty little daughter of yours?"

Rosa looked at her for a moment, a bit surprised by her question. "Which one do you mean? I have two daughters."

"The one with the pretty hair, the light one."

Rosa was offended. "Both of my daughters are pretty, thank you very much," she said.

The lady realized her mistake. "Oh, I didn't mean anything by it."

Ten years passed. Amore and Bella were inseparable, but Amore felt she would always have to protect Bella like a big sister. She knew that sometimes she was treated different than her sister. Amore would always get compliments about how pretty she was;

how her hair was so long and silky. Bella would ask Mr. Rogers questions about the cosmetics business, but for some reason, he always seemed to think Amore was more the business type. Amore would come up with ideas like lemonade stands to raise money for their Girl Scout uniforms. She was always full of ideas and very competitive, and she would tell Bella not to be afraid of a little competition, so Mr. Rogers started to show a lot of interest in Amore, and everyone else could see it as well.

Beth and Thomas were in their bedroom late one night. Beth looked at him. "I see Amore spends a lot of time in your office," she said.

Thomas smiled and replied, "Yes, that girl is not only beautiful, she is like a sponge. She soaks up information."

"Sounds like she is the son you never had," said Beth.

Thomas looked at her. "Do you have a problem with me spending time with Amore?" he asked.

Beth shook her head. She knew he had taken it negatively. "For heaven's sake, Thomas, no, I think that both of the girls look at you like a father. God only knows whatever happened to that sorry excuse of a biological father of theirs, and both girls need your attention," replied Beth.

Thomas said, "Bella stays to herself. She is not the same as Amore, and I don't know if she is going to have what it takes for the cosmetics business. She lacks decorum; she may not want to go to college."

"Thomas, they're twelve years old. It's too soon to talk about college, and what do you mean they're not the same?" said Beth.

"Yes, college, and if Bella wants to go, I will send them both, you know what I mean."

"You are such a great man, Thomas Rogers. But don't judge a book by its cover."

Thomas looked at her and sighed.

Five years flew by, and the girls were seniors in high school. Amore was accepted to Yale University. Bella was as well, but she decided to attend Spellman University in Atlanta.

Rosa and Bella were in the kitchen, talking. Rosa looked a bit tense for her daughter.

"Bella, why don't you want to go to Yale? It's such a great opportunity; it's an Ivy League school," she said.

"And Spellman is not a great school, is that what you're saying, mother?"

"No, that's not what I'm saying at all. What about your sister? You two have always been together. It's like you two are joined at the hip, and who is going to take care of you?" said Rosa.

"I don't need Amore to take care of me; I can take care of myself, and why am I always treated like I don't belong here?" Bella stormed out.

"I have to do something; I can't let them separate. They need each other," Rosa said to herself.

Later, Thomas was in the study on the phone, talking to his chief operations officer, Mr. Kellogg, about possibly selling parts of the company. Suddenly, Rosa came in, very upset.

"Rosa, what's the matter? What's going on?" asked Thomas.

"Thomas, we have to do something. We have to tell them the truth."

"For God sake, Rosa, lower your voice."

"I will not. I am tired of keeping quiet. The truth must come out. You have to tell the girls, Thomas, or I will."

"Let's just calm down a little here. Let's not do anything drastic."

"Drastic! The girls deserve the truth, and Beth deserves the truth, God please forgive me."

"Okay, I understand. Let's take a drive, and we can discuss this."

"No, we both will tell the girls that you are their father!"

"Do you have any idea what this will do? I love those girls. You know that this would destroy Beth and my marriage."

"Don't you think I know that? But all of these years keeping this secret. It has to end now!"

"Yes, you're right. Let me talk to Beth first. She has to know the whole truth, that it was something that just happened, that I love her and only her," said Thomas.

"It was a mistake between you and me, but those girls were not, and they need to know the truth. I will be leaving tonight; I wish things could have been different, Thomas. We both are at fault."

Outside the door, Bella had heard everything. She walked into the study. Rosa looked at her and said, "Hey, sweetheart, you came back."

"What's going on, Mother? Did I just hear what I thought I did?" asked Bella.

"Bella, try to understand."

"Shut up, Thomas! Mother, what's going on? Is this man my father?" asked Bella.

"Yes, Bella, he is your father."

Everyone looked at the door as Beth entered.

"Beth sweetheart, I can explain," said Thomas.

Beth looked at him, terrified. "Thomas! I have always known, the way you look at those girls and the way you treat Amore like the son you never had."

Rosa said, "Beth, I am so sorry. Please forgive me."

"I did a long time ago. You were a child, and I could never give Thomas any children, and I felt like how could I take that away from him," said Beth.

"We never meant to hurt you; we ended it before it ever began."

Beth hugged Rosa. "I think Bella is right. Maybe it's time she finds out for herself what she wants to do, not what anyone else wants. Even Amore," said Beth.

"Amore, I have to find her!" said Bella.

"Bella, wait, wait," said Rosa.

But, Bella went to find Amore to tell her about Thomas.

Finally, Bella found Amore in a restaurant. Amore was with a young man that she and Bella had gone to high school with by the name of Keith Washington. Keith was two years older than the girls and already attending college at Stanford University. Bella had always had a crush on Keith, but he had eyes for Amore. Keith and Amore were busy in their conversation as she reached them.

"Amore, I have been trying to call you," said Bella.

"My phone is off. What's wrong?" asked Amore.

"We have a problem," said Bella.

"Hello, Bella," said Keith.

"Hello, Keith, what are you doing in town?" asked Bella.

"I'm on break."

"Excuse me, Keith. What problem, Bella?" asked Amore.

"We need to go home now," was all Bella would say.

On their way home, Bella told Amore about Thomas being their father. Amore didn't seem to take the news the same as Bella. Amore felt that Thomas had always been there as a father. She was just upset at the fact that their parents didn't tell them from the beginning.

In his office, Amore confronted Thomas on why he didn't tell her about their relationship.

"You and my mom, and you never told me. All of the training and how I was so much like you when you were young, how I was like the son you never had, and this whole time you are my father, I don't understand." Amore was looking very upset as he tried to convince her.

"Your mother and I had an affair. We didn't think she would get pregnant. She didn't want to have an abortion, and neither did I, so we made up the Italian boyfriend. We gave you girls Italian names. I am so sorry; all I can do is make it up to you from this day forth, sweetheart. I love you and you are not the son I never had. You are my daughter."

"I love you too, Thomas," said Amore, with tears coming down her face.

"Can you call me Dad?"

"Yes!"

They embraced each other.

The girls headed off to college, but no, not together. Amore went off to Yale and Bella to Spellman.

While at Yale, Amore became a champion for women. She started Women of Empowerment, teaching women how to empower themselves through strength of the mind and heart, inspiration, wisdom, knowledge, positivity, innovation, stewardship, and the building of high self-esteem.

Keith Washington, the girls' old high school friend, continued to pursue Amore, but she was not interested. Keith was furious; he felt that Amore had led him on and wasted his time. So he reached out to Bella, who had diffidently came into her own. She had filled out and had the body of a goddess. She was at the top of her business class and head of her sorority.

Keith stopped by to visit her. "Bella, my, my. Have you grown up, girl. You look different."

"I look the same, Keith. What are you doing here?" asked Bella.

Keith smiled and replied, "I had to see you, I have been thinking about you. I just felt that when you go back home you'll work for your father."

"Excuse me, work for my father? No, that man is nothing to me. I'm not working for him, and what do you mean you've been thinking about me? I thought you were stuck on my sister."

"I dropped her a long time ago. I need a real Black woman."

He put his hand around her waist and got very close to her. "Plus, I have a proposition for you."

Bella didn't step back. "Proposition? And what's that, Mr. Washington?"

They hugged each other.

"Come work for me. I started a company about a year ago."

Bella smiled broadly. "You have your own company, wow!"

"I have some partners, silent partners, and we could use a smart up-and-coming gorgeous young lady like you," said Keith.

"What is it that you do, exactly?" asked Bella.

"We buy small companies in trouble and sell them, but we have a special job for you."

Meanwhile, Thomas called Amore and said he needed to see her at his office as soon as she got home from college.

"Hey Dad. Oh, I'm sorry, I didn't know you had a meeting," said Amore.

"Come on in, sweetheart. Mr. Kellogg was leaving. We will finish that conversation later, Bill," said Thomas.

"Okay, Thomas. Nice to see you again, Amore. Welcome home."

"Thanks, Mr. Kellogg. So what's the big emergency, Dad?"

"I have something to show you, so you come with me."

They walked down the hallway and stopped in front of a well-maintained office.

"This is your office," said Thomas.

"I thought this was Mr. Kellogg's office," said Amore.

Thomas smiled, looking at her. "Not anymore, now it belongs to the new COO."

"Are you kidding me, Dad? I just finished school. How can I be the COO?"

"I have been grooming you for this position ever since you were a little girl. You're ready."

"I don't know what to say! I promise, Dad, I won't let you down, but where is Mr. Kellogg moving? Are you stepping down?"

"No, you let me worry about Mr. Kellogg," said Thomas.

Meanwhile, Mr. Kellogg was on his cell phone with someone. "You were right. He gave her my position. That son of a bitch. All the years I gave him and that company. I will see that bastard in hell."

"Don't worry; he will get what's coming to him." Someone spoke from the other end.

Later, Amore was pleased about what she had received. She was sitting on the couch and decided to call Bella.

"Hey, where are you? Are you back home yet?"

Bella replied, "Yes, I'm at Mother's. Where are you?"

"I'm at Cee & Cee with Thomas, girl, and you will never guess what happened," said Amore.

"No, what? Did Keith ask you to marry him?" asked Bella.

"Keith, heavens no, why would you think that? That guy is nothing but trouble, Bella. Do yourself a favor and stay away from him. My news is that Thomas made me COO of the company."

"Congratulations, Amore, I know you always wanted to work side by side with Thomas."

Amore smiled. "So could you as well, Bella. We both are his daughters. He loves you just as much. Just give him a chance."

"Look, Amore, I love you very much, but you know we were always treated differently. That's the way the world has been for over 300 years, light skin vs. dark skin. Even more so in our race. Most Black celebrities that are admired for their beauty tend to have lighter complexions."

Amore replied, "This 'anti-Black' bias is evident in beauty standards and has caused self-hatred within the Black race. I understand that the solution to this problem is to educate Black children at an early age about their history and let them know that they are all beautiful boys and girls."

"Good luck with that. Amore! And good luck with your new position. really. Just remember, no matter what, I will always love you," said Bella.

"Why did you say it like that?" asked Amore.

"No special reason. I will see you later."

Bella ended the call and walked out of the room. She found Keith. He said, "Hello, sexy."

Bella told him the decision she made about his offer. "I'm in; I will take the position with your company."

"What about your sister? She'll be very angry."

Bella shook her head. "Collateral damage."

Amore got a call from her father.

"Amore, we have a problem," said Thomas.

Amore was confused. "What's going on?"

"Someone is buying up all the shares of the company. I am having an emergency board meeting as we speak. I need you back at the office as soon as possible."

"I'll be right there, but I have to make a stop first. I have an idea who could have done this," said Amore.

Amore headed directly to Keith's office. She had the feeling that Keith had something to do with the hostile takeover or would know something about it. Amore stormed into Keith's office, pushing the secretary out of the way.

"It's all right, Pam, let her in. I had an idea you would be coming by. I think you know everyone," said Keith.

Amore was shocked by what she was seeing. "Bella, Mr. Kellogg, Beth, what are you all doing here?"

"Meet my partners," said Keith.

Amore was stunned.

"What's wrong, Amore? Afraid of a little competition?" said Bella.

To be continued.

WRITTEN BY RICHARD DENNIS MAYS

CRISS CROSS

Marcus and Angela Jamison were high school sweethearts and very much in love. Marcus was a high school football and basketball star with many scholarship offers. Angela was the homecoming queen, the president of the school newspaper, and voted most likely to succeed; and both were voted most beautiful of their senior class. Shortly before graduating high school, Angela became pregnant. Marcus, trying to do the right thing, decided not to go to college and got a job at the local chicken plant. One year later, they were married. Marcus continued to work while Angela went to college at the state school. Angela graduated and began a small magazine company.

Angela was in the kitchen, reading the newspaper. Marcus entered and walked towards her. "Good morning, gorgeous." He kissed Angela on her cheek.

"Good morning, my handsome husband," said Angela. They both smiled, looking at each other.

"Guess what, we got the pre-approval for the magazine loan," said Angela.

"That's great, baby, when will you know the loan is approved?"

Angela nods. "Well, I have to talk with the loan officer," said Angela.

"That should not be a problem, babe. You have talked to loan officers before."

"Yeah, but this is the loan manager at the state bank."

"Angela, no other bank will pre-approve us."

"No, they are the only ones. Maybe Camel has changed."

Marcus sighed and said, "No, she hates us, Angela, she will never give us this loan."

"Baby, this loan will take the magazine to the next level, and you won't have to work at that awful chicken factory anymore," said Angela.

"It's a chicken plant, baby, not a factory," said Marcus.

"Plant, factory, whatever. It is not good."

"I know I know, baby. Camel will not make this easy," said Marcus.

"I have a meeting with her today at 3:00," said Angela.

Marcus nodded. He looked a bit tense. "Do you need me to go with you?"

"No, I think I should go by myself. We don't want to make it any worse," said Angela.

It was very clear that Camel, Marcus, and Angela had some past with each other.

Camel Sims went to high school with Marcus and Angela. Camel was not as popular in school. Her nickname was Camel the Hungry-Hungry Hippo. Marcus went out with Camel once as a favor to his sister. Camel took the date for more than it was. When Marcus and Angela started dating, Camel was furious and swore revenge on them.

And now Camel was the loan manager at the state bank. Camel was in her office, working. She was very well dressed, and her office was beautifully maintained. Her phone rang.

"Miss Sims, your 3:00 is here," said the receptionist.

Camel smiled broadly. "Send her in," she said.

After a few minutes, Angela walked in. "Hello Camel," said Angela.

Camel looked at her. "Well, if it isn't the homecoming queen."

"It's good to see you too, Camel. It's been a while," said Angela.

"Not since Marcus's father's funeral. Speaking of Marcus, where is that fine husband of yours?"

"I am not here to talk about Marcus, Camel, I am here to talk about the loan."

"The loan, yes, about that. I have some good news for you, homecoming queen. I approved the loan, and you have to sign the contract."

"Really, Camel? I don't know what to say," said Angela.

"Well, I need you to do something for me."

"What is it?"

"I have another contract for you to sign."

Angela looked confused by her reply. "Another contract?"

"Yes, it's for one night with your husband, Marcus."

"Is this some kind of a joke?" asked Angela.

"No joke. I want one night of passionate lovemaking with Marcus, and you are going to sign a contract stating you agree to it."

Angela burst out in anger, "What in the hell does this have to do with a bank loan, you crazy mental case bitch? You think I am going to let you sleep with my husband!"

Camel smiled. "Aw yeah, yes you will. You will, and you will sign this contract because you are used to getting everything you want, you high-yellow green-eyed bitch!"

"You take your contract, Camel, and you stick it up your fat ass!" Angela left the office. Camel laughed.

Angela got in her car and called Marcus and explained to him what happened. Marcus was furious and wanted to confront Camel, but Angela pleaded with him not to.

"What can we do? Why does she hate me so much? I never teased her or called her names in school. I even went out with her."

"Maybe that's the problem, I don't know. She hates me too, the way I look. She believes I am handed everything because of the way I look," said Angela.

"That could not be farther from the truth. You work harder than anyone I know. Doesn't she know how poor you were growing up?"

"No, and I don't think she cares. But, listen. I have an idea."

Angela called Marcus's brother Antwan. Antwan was the so-called playboy of the family. Angela believed she might be able to get Antwan to seduce Camel.

"What's up. It's Twan, baby," said Antwan.

"Antwan it's Angela."

"What's up baby girl, what's shakin'?"

"I need a big favor," said Angela.

"You know it ain't nothing but a word, baby girl. Whatcha need, baby girl?"

"You remember Camel Sims."

"Big dark-skinned girl, thick in the waist, pretty in the face," said Antwan.

"Aw yeah, I guess you could say that."

Angela filled Antwan in on the plan. Later, Antwan headed over to the bank to see Camel.

Camel was in her office as she received the call.

"Miss Sims, there is a Mr. Antwan Jamison to see you and he is very funny."

"Just send him in," said Camel.

Antwan entered the office. Camel looked at him.

"What's up, baby girl," he said.

Camel smiled. "Antwan Pretty Boy Jamison, what brings you here? You know you need more than a 300 hundred credit score to get a loan."

"Very funny, you got jokes. Anyway, I was in the area, and I just wanted to check you out, sweet thing," said Antwan.

"Really?"

"Yeah, baby girl, I saw you at the spot the other night. You were wearing that dress, lord have mercy. You know I like 'em thick in the hips and dark like chocolate chips."

Camel smiled, then said, "Why don't you bring your fine, smooth-talking self over here, come closer."

He got closer to her, and she whispered in his ear, "If you don't get your fake Shemar Moore ass out of my office, I will have security throw you out. And you tell your brother and your sister-in-law they best have their asses here to sign these contracts first thing in the morning or I have another surprise for them."

Marcus, Angela, and Antwan arrived at Camel's office the next morning. The plan was to confront Camel and tell her they will turn her in if she continued to blackmail them for the magazine loan. If she declined, they will no longer pursue the loan.

"Well, how is everyone doing this fine morning?" said Camel.

"If you were a man, I would beat the hell out of you." Marcus said.

"Such aggressiveness, I like that. Come on, beat my ass, baby."

"Camel, we came here for business, not your games. Can we get down to business, please?" said Angela.

"Sure, we can do that. Here are the pens. You can sign."

Antwan stopped her. "No one is signing anything here today, baby girl."

"Why is he talking?"

"Camel, we are not signing your contract, and Marcus will not be having sex with you," said Angela.

Marcus said, "That's right, I will never lower myself with the likes of you."

"Not only you, Mr. Marcus, but let's throw in fake playboy Antwan also, make it a threesome."

"Well," said Antwan.

"Shut up, Antwan. Camel, did you hear me? No!" said Angela.

"Marcus, you talk to your mother lately?"

"No, why are you asking about my mother?"

"I have a deed here with her name on it."

"Marcus, what is she talking about?" asked Angela.

"I can tell you," said Camel. "See, Ms. Jamison took out a second mortgage on the house after your father died."

"What the hell?" said Marcus.

Camel smiled. "The plot thickens."

"Camel, you can't be that god awful."

"Camel, you know my mother, she never hurt you."

"Look, beautiful people. This is the deal. You are going to sign these contracts, your mother will get her house back, and everyone will live happily ever after."

"Angela, what can we do? My mother?" said Marcus.

"You win Camel, but only if you sweeten the pot." said Angela.

Camel looked surprised by her sudden change. "What do you mean?"

"No interest for the first two years and double the loan."

"I can't do that!"

"Sure you can, you're the loan manager. Everyone loves you."

Marcus and Angela signed the contracts. Camel kissed Marcus and Antwan on the cheek and told Angela, "Great doing business with you."

They left the bank, walking swiftly. Camel leaned back in her desk chair and laughed.

"Great job, baby, she didn't have a clue," said Marcus.

"Yeah, you played her smooth, baby girl, great plan." Antwan added.

"Yeah, she thought we didn't know about your mother's house. She fell right into our trap. She had no idea we were going to sign the contracts anyway. I would love to see the look on her face when she finds out that we're swingers, and we enjoy different partners."

"Maybe you can join us, baby."

"Maybe I will, I like them thick in the hips and dark like chocolate chips."

Marcus and Angela went on to have a great life. The magazine became one of the largest in the country, and Marcus started working for the magazine writing for the sports section and finally left the chicken plant. Antwan was still the town playboy and smooth-talking all the ladies. Camel continued as the loan officer for the state bank and was still bitter; her revenge wasn't as sweet as she thought it would be. However, there would always be old high school classmates to get revenge on.

THE END

WRITTEN BY RICHARD DENNIS MAYS

DEAD MAN'S CURVE

The year was 1983. Two teenage boys were driving home after playing their rival school in a high school football game. Michael was the star quarterback, and his best friend Josh was all state linebacker. The boys ran out of gas near dead man's curve and had to walk to the nearest gas station. Both of them were very intoxicated.

"Hey dude, I thought you said we had enough gas to make it home," said Josh.

Michael looked at him and said, "A quarter of a tank would normally get me back. I misjudged it, dude."

"We only have a couple of miles to get to the gas station. Grab that gas can out of the truck for me," said Michael.

"The only thing you misjudged was how many beers you had," said Josh.

Michael laughed. "I only had a twelve pack."

"Yeah right. Hey, is that someone walking?"

Michael looked at where Josh was looking. "Yeah, it looks like some man coming toward us. Wait, where did he go?"

"He disappeared, what the hell!" said Josh.

Michael said, with fear in his voice, "There he goes again, what is he? Looks like he's floating."

"Let's get the hell out of here."

Simultaneously both of them started running. They made it to the gas station. Michael called his father from the phone booth at the station and asked him to pick them up. Michael and Josh were not sure if they should tell anyone what they had seen for fear no one would believe them. However, when Michael and his father got home, Michael's father asked him if he had been drinking. That's when Michael definitely knew his father would not believe his ghost story. The next day, after he picked up his truck, Michael went to see his grandfather. He got out of the car, then walked to the door. He sighed and then knocked.

"Grandpa."

"Come on in, Michael. What brings you over here this time of the morning?"

Michael looked around a bit, then replied, "Josh and I ran out of gas last night by dead man's curve. I just picked up my car."

"Dead man's curve, you kids need to be very careful driving out there."

"Why do they call it dead man's curve anyway, Grandpa?" asked Michael.

Grandpa sighed and then said, "Because of the number of people killed in that area with no survivors. In some cases they never even found the bodies. The police claimed maybe their bodies were missing because of the swamp and the alligators may have eaten them. The weird thing is, the swamp is miles away from the curve."

"That is crazy. Josh and I saw something walking by the curve last night, we think."

Grandpa looked surprised. "What do you mean you think?"

"This is going to sound even more crazy, Grandpa. It looked like a man and he was floating."

"Was he wearing a white shirt and black pants?" asked Grandpa.

Michael was shocked to hear that. "Yes, how did you know that?"

"A long time ago, when I was a young boy, my grandfather would tell me stories about a man with a white shirt and black pants walking near that curve," says Grandpa.

"Is it the ghost of one of the people killed on that curve?"

"No, my grandfather told me the man is guarding his treasure."

Again Michael was shocked. His eyes got bigger. "Treasure!!!!"

Grandpa nodded. "The story is that a long, long time ago, people didn't put their treasures or money in a bank, they buried it or hid it somewhere. And if they died without telling anyone where it was, their spirit would guard the treasure for eternity or until someone found it."

Michael looked a bit confused. "What happens then?"

"The spirit gets to finally rest and the treasure will belong to the person who finds it," said Grandpa.

"Grandpa, you're telling me that there is treasure at that curve and some spirit is just trying to scare people away from it?"

"That's the story my grandfather told me. Michael, you kids stay away from that curve, don't let the story of treasure consume you. Remember, money is the root of all evil."

Michael thought for a moment. "Yeah, sure thing Grandpa, we will start going the back way through the town of St. Paul," said Michael. "See you later, Grandpa."

"Remember what I said, Michael."

"Yes…"

Michael walked out the door. His intentions were different after hearing all that from his grandfather.

Later, Michael stopped by Josh's house and told Josh everything his grandfather told him. Josh thought there was still a logical explanation for this;

maybe they did have too much to drink. Michael told Josh they were going to tell only their girlfriends about the treasure, and tonight they were going treasure hunting. At nightfall, Michael and Josh got their older friend Tommy to buy some beer for them, and then they picked up their girlfriends, Sydney and Shannon. Michael told the girls the story. They laughed and thought it was just boys being boys and went along with the treasure hunt.

Then Michael noticed Shannon's outfit.

"Hey, why are you girls all dressed up? I said to wear old clothes; we're going to be digging for treasure," said Michael.

Shannon shook her head. "Whatever. Are you guys serious? There is no ghost and no treasure; I thought we were just going out."

"Yes, there is treasure and we are going to find it tonight. We all are going to be rich," said Michael.

"I am not sure about this, Michael. What about the ghost in the white shirt, dude?"

"He won't do anything, I think he is just walking around to scare people away. We will be fine. No worries, dude."

Sydney got closer to Josh and said, "What is going on with Michael? He doesn't seem like himself."

Josh replied, "Come on dude, lets head back. This is crazy."

Michael looked at Josh. "Josh, you and I have been friends forever, dude, have I ever led you wrong? I promise you guys if anything strange starts to happen we leave, okay?"

The car stopped and all of them got out. "We're here, get the shovels and flashlights," said Michael.

"It's so dark out here, no streetlights at all. I can't see a thing," said Sydney.

"Here Sydney, take this flashlight. Stay close to me," said Josh.

"Everyone follow me. The spirit, ghost or whatever the hell, he was walking close to the end of the curve."

"My mother told me there used to be a house here when she was a little girl and that it was built in the eighteen hundreds," said Shannon.

"That's it if we can find out where the house was," said Michael.

Suddenly, Sydney fell over something.

"Sydney, are you okay?"

Sydney looked like she was in pain. "No, I fell and hurt my ankle."

Using his flashlight, Josh looked for whatever had tripped Sydney. "It looks like some old steps."

"That's it. Let's start digging here, this is the spot," said Michael.

"Get down!"

"What is it?" asked Shannon.

"It's him, he's coming, get down," said Josh.

"Oh my God, oh my God I see him."

Michael was very keen. "Keep digging! He can't do anything, he's just a spirit," said Michael.

"He's coming this way." Shannon started running.

Sydney was right behind her. "Shannon, let's hide behind these bushes."

They were both very frightened. "He's coming this way."

Meanwhile, Michael continued to dig. Finally he hit something. The spirit was moving closer to Shannon and Sydney, but he headed back towards Michael and Josh as they found the treasure.

Michael told Josh to help him with the object in the hole. It looked like an old trunk. Michael broke open the old rusty lock.

"Wow! Unbelievable, dude," said Michael.

Josh looks at him. "What is it? What is it?"

"A trunk full of gold bars and coins. We did it," said Michael.

Josh looked up to see Shannon and Sydney running towards them. As soon as he turned around, the spirit grabbed Josh by the throat. Josh looked in the creature's face. It was partly melted like it had been burned off. One eye and part of the chin was missing. He put his large hand over Josh's face and squeezed his head until it popped like a grape and then he ate his brains. The girls were screaming and crying, wanting to run but frozen in fear. Michael was hiding in the hole with the treasure, and the girls were pleading for their life.

"Please, please don't kill us," sobbed Sydney. The spirit looked at the girls with snakes coming out of his eyes. "We don't want your treasure, please let us go."

The spirit hovered over the girls.

"Over here! Over here!" called Michael. He tried to distract him. Screaming from the hole, as the spirit started toward him, he yelled, "Come get me, you ugly fuck!"

The spirit got into the hole and pulled Michael and the treasure in with him as they both disappear into the hole. The girls were lost and could not find their way out of the woods. They were screaming for help but no one could hear them.

The next morning, Michael's father received a call from the police. They found Michael's truck by dead man's curve. When his father arrived, there were three dead bodies covered with white sheets.

"What happened?" asked Michael's dad.

The chief police officer said, "Looks like they were drinking and hit the curve too fast and crashed into a tree."

The chief looked at the bodies and back again to him. "Sorry, but we still have not found your son Michael's body. My men are still looking. My guess right now is maybe alligators or something from that swamp."

Tears started to fall from the father's eyes.

"What was he wearing?" asked the chief.

"His number twelve red and white football jersey and some blue jeans."

The chief nodded.

"Who was in the car with him?" asked Michael's dad.

"Josh Francis, Shannon Bridgman, and Sydney Sharpe. Their parents are on the way."

Thirty years passed. Across from dead man's curve was a new housing complex. One night some kids from the complex decided to camp out at the curve inside the woods. They had heard stories about the spirit that walks the curve, guarding his treasure. That night the kids saw the spirit walking toward them. They ran out of the woods and jumped in their car. The spirit stood in front of the car with snakes coming out of his eyes. He wore a red and white number twelve football jersey.

THE END

STORY NO. 5:

WRITTEN BY RICHARD DENNIS MAYS

FAMILY AFFAIR

Eddie, Ann, their nephew Mike, and some friends were having a party that included alcohol and drugs. Eddie didn't indulge in alcohol or drugs like his wife Ann. Eddie had to go to work later that night; he was a manager at a supermarket warehouse in the city. Mike was Eddie's brother's son and he lived with them. He was sixteen years old and Eddie was his favorite uncle. Eddie and Ann let Mike's high school friends hang out over at their house from time to time, mostly his best friend Tony.

"Sweetheart, it's almost 11:00, time for me to head out of here," said Eddie.

Ann called from the bathroom, "Okay baby, I will see you in the morning."

Mike was outside smoking a cigarette, seeing his friend Tony off. Eddie told Mike to call him at work and let him know if Eddie Jr got out of bed, that Ann would let him get up and watch movies late. Mike put out the cigarette and watched his uncle drive off. He returned to the house, sat down on the couch and poured a drink of vodka; then Eddie Jr. came in the room.

"Mike, where is my mama?" asked Eddie Jr.

Mike looked at him. "She is in the bathroom, little man; your dad said you must stay in bed."

"I want some water!"

"No, go back to bed, Eddie Jr. I am going to call your dad. You can't have water; you'll wet the bed," said Mike.

Eddie Jr returned to bed. Mike continued to drink his vodka and rolled up a joint. Ann was still in the bathroom taking a shower, getting ready for bed. Ann came out of the bedroom into the living room wearing a short black Victoria's Secret negligee, not covering much at all. She put her left foot on top of the coffee table in front of Mike and pulled her underwear to the side.

"What are you doing?" asked Ann.

"I am drinking this vodka and about to light up this joint, you want some?"

"I think I've had too much already. I want to do other things."

"I told you, I cannot keep doing that. You're married to my uncle, it's not right." He was staring between her legs.

"You're telling me you don't want this? Come on and do it like I taught you," said Ann.

Mike started to give Ann oral sex while her leg was propped up on the coffee table; Ann guided Mike's head while he pleasured her with his tongue. Ann led Mike to the bedroom. Halfway down the hall, Mike picked up Ann and carried her into the bedroom. Once in the bedroom, Ann started to take off Mike's clothes.

"I love you so much," said Mike.

"I love you too."

"Every time I try to stop, I can't. What have you done to me, it's like we have the same DNA. I cannot get you out of my head."

Ann smiled broadly. Both of them were lost in their lust. "I am showing you a real woman, not those little girls you are normally with," she said.

Suddenly, there was a knock at the back door. Mike jumped out of the bed and hid in the closet. Ann went to the door. "Who is it?" she asked.

"It's me, Fred, is it clear?" Fred was Eddie's sister's husband.

Then Mike came out of the closet and yelled, "What's up man?"

"Hey Mike, is Eddie home?"

"No man, he at work," replied Mike.

"Okay, I will talk to him tomorrow."

Fred left as Mike looked at Ann. "Why would Fred be looking for Eddie this time of night and coming to the back door?"

"I don't know baby, come on back to bed."

"Are you sleeping with Fred? And what is going on between you and Tony?"

She shook her head.

"I saw you in the car with him the other day," said Mike.

She knew how to handle the sixteen year old. "Do you love me?"

Mike sighed and replied, "Yes, you know I do."

"Then stop worrying about things you don't need to worry about."

Mike and Ann fell asleep after making love all night. The next mornng, there was a noise at the front door. It was Eddie.

"Mike, get up! Get up!"

"What?"

"Eddie is home, hide, get in the closet! He is coming in."

She walked out and found Eddie.

"You're up early," he said.

"I heard you coming in, baby. Why don't you take a shower and get in bed. I'll put fresh linen on the bed for you," replied Ann.

While Ann and Eddie were in the front room talking, Mike sneaked down the hall into his room.

"You don't have to do that, baby," said Eddie.

Ann smiled. "It's not a problem, baby."

"Where is Mike, still in bed?"

"Yeah, I think he was up late. I went to bed when you left. He was still up."

Eddie sighed and realized something. "I don't know what I would do without you, baby. Thanks for taking care of my nephew and letting him stay with us."

"It's my pleasure, sweetheart," replied Ann.

Eddie smiled as they both walked down the hall. Eddie was unaware of what was going on in the family. He was thinking that his wife was the best thing he ever had. But his mentality would change. Six months later, Eddie found out that Ann was cheating on him with the neighbor and divorced her. He never found out about his nephew or the others, or he never said anything if he did. Mike was never with her again, but she would always have a part of him.

THE END

DEPENDENT

David was in the kitchen. He was making breakfast, taking out the trash, cleaning up. He was completely absorbed in his work. Alison entered, dressed for work. "Good morning, baby."

David smiled at her. "Good morning sunshine," he said.

Alison kissed David on the cheek, showing their love and affection.

"That smells good, but I am going to have to take it with me. Early morning, I have to drive to Ft. Worth for Perry. I won't get to the office until late afternoon. Where is Jazzy?"

"She already left. Ms. Simmons picked her up so she could ride to school with Pamela."

"Those two girls have been friends since the second grade."

"Actually, since kindergarten they have been best friends, babe."

Alison smiled and nodded. "Oh yeah."

"It's going to be crazy this time of the morning," said David.

"I know a few back roads."

"You must have had a long night at the office again."

Alison nodded and replied, "I did, we were trying to finish the quarterly report. The numbers come out today, and Perry feels this may be our best numbers in the company's history."

She kisses and hugs him. "You were sleeping so good when I came in and I didn't want to wake you."

David smiled as if he had something different to say. "I have some great news."

"What is it? Don't keep me in suspense."

"I got the supervisory job at the shipyard," said David.

"Oh my God, congratulations baby. I know how much you wanted that position, I am so happy for you."

"Frank, the regional manager, said in the next two years, I have an opportunity to become a manager with my military experience and all. Now I can start paying for some things around here and not have to depend on my executive, sexy, six-figure-plus wife having to pay for everything."

She sighed. "David, I don't mind paying, and I don't pay for everything. I know how hard you work and take care of everything around here. I know you want to buy me wonderful extravagant things, take me out to fancy restaurants, but I don't care about those things. We are a team, baby; it doesn't matter who makes more money. I love you."

"I love you too, baby. Hey, what about the COO position, you think you're going to get it?" asked David.

Alison thought a bit. "Maybe. I should be next in line since Mr. Barnes announced his retirement.

Perry has been hinting around lately, but you never can tell."

"Well, he should know, he is the CEO. All that work and long hours you put into that company! If you don't get that position, Perry and I are going to have a problem, CEO or not."

"Thanks for having my back, baby. I should get on the road now, I may be a little late tonight. You can start dinner without me." She kissed him.

David smiled, looking at her. "Like always, have a wonderful day."

The main road was bustling. On the side of the road, there was a big, impressive building. It was the headquarters for the M and M Marketing Group.

Alison walked into the office. There was a celebration going on. She made her way over to Gail, her co-worker and best friend. "Gail, what's going on?"

"The numbers came in early this morning for the quarter, the biggest ever, so Perry is celebrating with all the staff. Sebastian, Perry's personal assistant, told me he thinks that Perry will call you in and offer you the COO position."

Alison was silent and surprised too.

"He has been raving about how instrumental you have been in this monumental quarter we've had, and you know how Perry is. You deserve that position, girl, let me be the first to congratulate you," said Gail.

Alison smiled. "Thanks, Gail." They hugged.

"Oh, David got the supervisor position," said Alison.

"He did? That's great. I know he has been waiting for a long time."

While Alison and Gail talked, Lori and Valerie were having a conversation on the other side of the room. Lori always thought she should get the COO position because of her credentials and family name.

"Hey girl," said Valerie.

"What?" asked Lori.

"I heard Alison is getting the COO position, and Perry is going to tell her today," said Valerie.

"I knew it. She has always been kissing up to that little troll Perry. She is so pathetic, like a little dog wagging its tail."

Both of them headed over to Gail and Alison.

"Guess who is coming up behind you?" asked Gail.

"Who?"

"Your arch enemy, Lori. And Valerie is with her."

"Hey sister, hey girl," said Lori.

Alison replied before Gail. "What's up, Lori, hello Valerie."

"I hear congratulations are in order," said Lori.

"For what?"

"A little birdie told me that you're our new COO."

Alison looked at Valerie. "Well, that little birdie told you wrong."

"Sorry if I was premature," Lori said.

"I am sure you are, Lori."

Gail grabbed Alison's arm. "Lori, can you excuse us? We were having a private conversation," she said.

"Okay, see you ladies later. Enjoy the party." Lori started walking away. "I hate that bitch...." she said.

Alison heard it. "I hate that bitch!"

"Girl, don't pay any attention to her, don't let her take away your positive energy. Let's get back into the now. Where were we? Oh, you were telling me about David," said Gail.

"Yes, David has been waiting a long time, girl. I don't know what he will do if something happens to that job. I want to see Perry, is he in his office?"

"Yes, but I think he has someone in there. Ask Sebastian and find out who it is."

Alison found Sebastian.

"Alison, how are you doing? Something is not right. Perry is keeping everything on the hush, girl, close to the vest," said Sebastian.

"So you don't know who is in the office with Perry."

"Between you and me, I think it's the new COO. Sorry, girl," said Sebastian.

Alison knocked on Perry's door.

"Come in."

She walked inside. "Perry, are you busy?"

"There she is, come on in, superstar."

Perry came from behind his desk to meet her. "I would like you to meet someone, Alison. This is Mr. Joseph Okafor. Mr. Okafor is going to be the new COO, he is from the Chicago office," said Perry.

"It's such a pleasure to finally meet you, Alison. I've heard so many great things about you," said Mr. Okafor.

Looking at Perry, Alison said, "Thank you, but I have not heard anything about you."

"Excuse me, but are you from New York?" asked Mr. Okafor.

"No, but I lived there for a while. I went to Columbia Business School."

"Oh yes, that's where I remember you from! But your last name wasn't Williams then."

Alison replied, "No, it was Hayes. You went to Columbia?"

"A long time ago as a student, but I taught there when you were there," said Mr. Okafor.

"Dr. Sims' class, now I remember. Small world."

"Yes, indeed," said Mr. Okafor.

Both of them smiled as Perry grabbed Mr. Okafor's arm and hugged him while walking him to the door.

"Joseph, I will see you bright and early Monday morning."

He nodded and replied, "Yes sir, Mr. Johnson!"

"Call me Perry, everyone else does," said Perry.

"Again, it's been a pleasure to see you again, Mrs. Williams. Hope to see you on Monday."

"Nice seeing you again as well, and congratulations on the promotion," said Alison.

"Thank you," said Mr. Okafor. Finally, he left the office.

"Before you say anything let me explain, please. Have a seat, please."

Alison continued to stand with arms folded.

"I know you were expecting the COO position, but we have bigger plans for you, my dear. The board and I recognize all the hard work you've put into this company. That's why you are the new CEO of the Los Angeles office."

He poured two mimosas and offered one to her. "Let's toast your new position!"

"What? Perry, don't mess with me," said Alison.

"Congratulations, young lady, you have earned it."

"Perry, I don't know what to say."

Perry smiled and nodded. "Well, I know you won't let me down. You are going to do great things in LA. So, take the rest of the day off and tell your family the great news. We will talk about the details Monday," said Perry.

"Perry, thank you so much for this opportunity, and I promise I won't let you down." She hugged him and left the office.

Gail was on the office floor, talking with Mr. Barnes.

"Gail, I am going to miss you," said Mr. Barnes.

They hugged. "I will miss you too, Mr. Barnes. So what are you going to do now, Mr. Retired?" asked Gail.

"Going to get in my boat and hit that water."

"Fishing?"

"Yeah, and maybe a little consulting on the side if I get bored. Excuse me, there's Jacob. I need to see him. Let me talk to you later, Gail."

Gail kissed him on his cheek. "Okay, if I don't see you, have a happy retirement," she said.

Alison came straight to Gail.

"What happened, did you get it?" asked Gail.

Alison was very excited. "No! I didn't, they picked someone from the Chicago office, and I knew him, well kind of, he went to Columbia. It's a long story, but guess what, they picked me to run the LA office," said Alison.

"What? Running the LA office, are you saying that they made you the CEO?"

Her voice was low as no one could hear.

"Yes! Girl, this is so amazing, I can't believe it."

"Have you told David yet?"

Her excitement turned to concern. "David? Oh my God, David."

Suddenly she was lost in a dream. She imagined she was about to tell David.

David came home from work. Alison had made a candlelight dinner for two, so she could break the news about moving to LA.

"Hey babe, what's going on? Why are you home so early? Did you get the COO job?" asked David.

"No, have a seat, sweetheart," said Alison.

David stopped for a second. "Wait a minute; something doesn't feel right. Where is Jazzy? You haven't made dinner like this in a long time."

"Jazzy is staying the night at Pamela's so we can be alone."

"But if you didn't get the COO job, what are we celebrating? Why did you make this dinner?" asked David.

"Perry and the board selected me as the CEO of the LA office."

"What? LA as in California? Wait, they made you the CEO and are moving you across the country and we didn't even discuss it?"

"What is there to discuss babe? I will be making about $400,000 a year, double what I am making now," said Alison.

"So, I don't have any say about what happens in this family?" asked David.

"No, honey, that's not what I am saying at all." She rubbed his arm.

"So, let me get this straight. You want me to quit my job, which I just got the supervisor position, take Jazzy out of school, leave our family and friends so we can move across the damn country for your promotion."

"David, this is a great opportunity for our entire family."

David said angrily, "You always control everything in this family. You think because you make more money than me, I have no say in this house. I never feel any self-worth. I didn't get a Bachelor's degree from the University of Texas and go to business school at Columbia like you. I only have a high school diploma, but I am still your husband and the man of this house."

Alison tried to calm him down.

"No, get your hands off me. That's what's wrong with this country. Women want to be men; men want to be women."

"David, I appreciate everything you do. I don't want to walk in your shoes, I am not trying to compete with you. I understand your struggle," said Alison.

"What did you say, you understand my struggle?" asked David.

"David, I..."

"Shut the hell up." David pushed the dinner and everything off the table. "You shut your mouth when I am talking. I go to work, come home and cook, take care of Jazzy when she is sick, help her with her homework, and spend time with her. While you're working late nights and away on business trips."

"David, why didn't you tell me you had a problem with my career," said Alison.

"Shut up!" He pointed his finger in her face. She was frightened. "I have to be dependent on you. What kind of man are you if you have to depend on a woman."

David stormed out the door.

"David, David!" called Alison. She ran after him.

"Alison, Alison, did you hear what I said?"

Alison came out of her daydream. "I was thinking about how I will tell David we're moving to California," she said.

"Well, you know your husband better than I do. I do know this about David. He loves you very much. Just remember that."

"You're right, girl, and I will let you know how it goes."

Alison was home, waiting for David. The house was well maintained, and dinner was ready. It was all for him.

David came in. "Hey, you're home early." He noticed everything. "What is this fancy dinner about? Did you get the position?"

"Something like that."

David looked a bit surprised. "Uh oh, what's going on, baby?" he asked.

"I got a better position. You may wanna sit down. I am just going to say it. They offered me the CEO position, but in the Los Angeles office."

He was silent.

"Before you say anything, baby, this is what we have been working so hard for. Look, I know you just got the supervisor position."

"Alison, Alison, this is great news, baby. I am so proud of you." He got up and hugged her.

"You aren't angry?"

"Why would I be angry? Baby, I know you, I treasure you. You are number one in my life. You deserve that position because you worked your ass off."

Alison was surprised. "You're not disappointed about leaving your job?"

David smiled. "I will find another job. Whereever you go, I go."

He kissed Alison. "I love you so much!"

Alison was in tears. "I love you too…"

Six months later, Alison and Gail were lying by the hotel pool in Los Angeles, drinking mimosas.

"This is the life. Thank you so much for giving me this opportunity," said Gail.

Alison looked at Gail. "Congratulations, new COO of the LA office," said Alison.

THE END

LOVE TRIANGLE

Ben, the top insurance agent for the Mainstay Insurance Company, walked in one morning. Olivia was on the phone but saw Ben as he entered and smiled at him. The office manager, Susan, was going to let Ben know that he was promoted to manager and would be transferred to the New York office in Manhattan.

"Good morning, Ben," said Susan.

Ben replied with a smile. "Good morning, Susan."

"Come over to my desk."

"What's going on?" Ben sat down across from her.

"You got it. You got the promotion."

Ben was surprised. "What, you're kidding me. I'm moving upstairs or what?"

"That's the other part, it's the New York office," said Susan.

"I said I'd go anywhere, but that was a year ago."

"You think your wife would have a problem?" asked Susan.

Ben shook his head. "No, she would love New York, that's not it," said Ben.

"We'll talk to Mrs. Simmons in human resources; she will fill you in on everything. I just had to give you a heads up on the great news," said Susan.

"Thanks, Susan." Ben walked to his desk. He looked a bit disappointed.

Everyone in the office came over to Ben's desk to congratulate him. Wanda, who was new to the office. Gwen, who had been there for fifteen years. Olivia, who was Ben's best friend in the office; and Sheldon, who thought he was getting the promotion but was really never considered.

"Congrats, man, I knew you were going to get it, dawg. I was in line for it, but I told them I had too much on my plate already," said Sheldon.

"Yeah, thanks."

"Haven't known you very long, but it has been fun, you make everyone laugh. Congratulations, and good luck in New York," said Wanda.

"Thanks, Wanda, you're going to love it here."

"Congratulations, and you keep in touch ya hear, or I will have somebody drive me up there and beat you, you understand?" said Gwen.

Ben nodded. "Yes, ma'am, I understand now," he said.

Olivia was last in line. "Congratulations, big brother, I'm going to miss you so much."

"I'm going to miss you as well, little sis, you have no idea how much. Before I forget, tell that husband of yours to call me, maybe we can get a few holes in on the golf course."

"He's out of town again on business, he didn't tell you?" said Olivia.

"Oh, yeah, maybe he did."

"I've been so busy with the kids and working so many hours lately. Can you call me later tonight?

I have something very important to tell you," said Olivia.

"Sure thing, I'm home by myself anyway. Pam went to Vegas with her sisters. It's her birthday; they planned the trip months ago," said Ben.

"Really? I saw her in the store last week and she didn't mention she was going to Vegas. I hope she has fun."

"I'm sure she will, her sisters seem more important to her sometimes than me."

Later, Sheldon rolled his chair over to Ben. Ben was surprised to see him again.

"Hey, dawg," said Sheldon. "How much does that manager position pay?"

"I'm not sure, bro, I haven't talked numbers yet."

"I was just checking, just in case they give a brother a call," said Sheldon.

Later that evening, Ben was thinking he had not heard anything from his wife, Pam. He looked at his phone for the text he thought she sent him that morning with her hotel information. The text only read love you, call you when I get there. Ben called her cell phone.

She wasn't picking up the call, so he decided to leave a voice mail for her.

"Hey baby, just wanted to see if you made it safe. I don't have your hotel information. Give me a call soon as you get this, I have some great news for you."

He just finished the message when his phone rang. On the other end was Olivia.

"What happened, you didn't call me?"

"I was trying to get in touch with Pam, and I don't have any of her information. I totally forgot to call you, I'm sorry," said Ben.

"Ben, why are you acting surprised? She does that to you all the time, why do you put up with it?"

"The same reason you put up with Franklin's mess. I love her," said Ben.

"You're right, Ben, we both put up with a lot. I do love Franklin, but sometimes that's not enough."

Ben was surprised to hear it. "What do you mean?"

"Are you happy?" asked Olivia.

"With Pam? She is the mother of my children. She has a great job."

"Nevertheless, are you happy? Do you laugh together, are you friends?" asked Olivia.

Ben shook his head. "Are you happy?"

"No, I am not. Ben, I mean no disrespect to your marriage and definitely not to mine, but since the first time I met you, I've felt an attraction, and as I got to know you more, I really felt it."

He was silent.

"I'm so honored to have met you, and working with you has been awesome. I always looked forward to coming into work, and I got a little gitty whenever I would get close to you, but I knew how to play it cool."

Finally Olivia stopped. Then Ben spoke. "This is so crazy. I feel the same way. I have been wanting to tell you the same things for a long time, that's why I have had mixed emotions about leaving for New York. Olivia, I wish you and your husband the very best, but I cannot stop thinking about you. We always have so much fun, and we are best friends. Olivia, you brought me sunshine when I only saw rain; you brought me laughter when I only felt pain," said Ben.

"It's like you can't fight who you are attracted to. It's crazy because I'm blessed with my family, and I have a very good man, but all in all, from day one, I've been attracted to you," said Olivia.

"Are you sure it's not because Franklin is always away on business?"

"No, he has gone out of town on long business trips way before I ever met you, and I've never felt this way about anyone else," said Olivia.

"Yeah, Pam has always gone on trips with her sisters or friends. Have you heard from Franklin?" asked Ben.

"No, but that's nothing new."

"Where was his business trip again?"

"Hold up, let me recheck this email."

"Yeah…"

"Las Vegas?"

"What? He's in Vegas also?" said Ben.

Ben continued to try to call Pam and Olivia continued to try to reach Franklin, but they had no luck. The next morning Olivia called Franklin's boss, and he told her Franklin was not in Las Vegas. He was in the Dominican Republic, where the company had an office. Franklin had been working out of that office for over ten years. Franklin's boss gave Olivia Franklin's phone number at that office.

Olivia called that phone number.

"Hello," said an unknown female voice with a Dominican accent.

"Yes, I'm looking for Franklin Myers."

"Franklin's not here right now. May I ask who is calling," the woman replied.

"His wife."

"There must be some mistake. I am his wife."

In shock, Olivia told the unknown woman about her marriage to Franklin, that they have three kids. The woman tells Olivia she has been married to Franklin for almost ten years and has two kids by him.

Later, Ben finally heard from Pam. "You've been trying to reach me?"

Ben sighed. "Yeah, are you okay?" asked Ben.

"I am fine, Ben. Ben, I have something to tell you, and before you go crazy, just listen to me."

"Go crazy? Pam, what's going on?" asked Ben.

"I have been seeing someone else, but it's not what you think."

Ben was confused. "You are seeing someone else, and I'm supposed to think what? Is this some kind of joke?"

"See you're not listening, that's the problem with you. It's a woman, I knew her in high school. We always had these feelings for each other. Therefore, I am letting you know that this is my life now, and I'm leaving you. Now, do you have anything to say?"

Ben was shocked. He wasn't able to say anything.

"Ben…"

He simply hung up the phone.

Six months later, Franklin was living in the Dominican Republic with his Dominican wife. Olivia divorced him and never turned him into the authorities. She told him to stay away from her and their children. Pam and her high school sweetheart were married and moved to Los Angeles. As for Ben, he never took the promotion to New York. He took the promotion upstairs, moved in with Olivia, and asked her to marry him, and she said yes. So, the only trips they take were together and with the kids.

Friends accept your past, support your present, and encourage your future.

THE END

WRITTEN BY RICHARD DENNIS MAYS

PROGRAMMED

Regina James was a seventeen-year-old girl living with her mother in a two-bedroom apartment with two older sisters, a younger brother, and a baby sister. Her mother was a single parent, and her name was Missy.

"Regina! Regina!" called Missy.

"Yeah!"

"What did you say?" asked Missy.

"Yes, Mama."

"I thought so. What were you doing?"

"My homework."

"You don't have time for that; you need to watch your baby sister. I am going out for a while," said Missy.

Regina was sad. "Why do I always have to watch her, Mama? I was doing my homework."

"You think that's going to help you get away from here? Your sister Mary graduated from high school and look where she's at. She's a crackhead, steals everything that's not bolted down. You just do what I tell you."

Regina nodded. "Yes Mama."

Regina's oldest sister Jasmine walked out of the bedroom. Jasmine had two kids of her own, but they were taken away by child services. Jasmine was on crack cocaine, but was trying to get herself together in order to get her kids back. Jasmine also suffered from sickle cell anemia and had been battling it since childhood.

"Hey booger rat, did Mama get her food stamps yet?" asked Jasmine.

Regina looked at her. "Would you please stop calling me booger rat?"

"It's just a nickname, Regina, stop being such a baby."

"I don't know why Mama never asks you to watch Latoya."

"You think Mama is going to trust me with a baby? Why she still having babies anyway? She has grandkids."

"So I can babysit. Have you found a job yet?" asked Regina.

"No, I did everything they wanted me to do. I got my GED; I am clean off the drugs, staying off the street. Still no one will give me a chance."

"Mama said getting an education wouldn't help anyone get out of here anyway," said Regina.

"Maybe she's right."

Later that night Missy came home with a new friend, Curtis. Regina was asleep with the baby on the couch. Their brother Travis was asleep on a mattress on the floor. Missy took Curtis to her bedroom.

Next day in the early morning, the baby was crying. Regina was trying her best.

Missy came out of her bedroom. "Regina, keep her quiet. Curtis is trying to sleep."

"She is hungry, Mama. Who is Curtis?"

"Just put some rice in her bottle with the milk and keep her quiet. I told Curtis she was yours anyway." She closed the bedroom door.

Travis woke up. Travis was fifteen years old and the only male in the family. Travis felt it was his responsibility to take the role as the man of the house, when no one ever taught him how to be a man.

Regina asked, "Travis, where have you been for two days?"

"Taking care of my business." He pulled out a roll of money. Regina was surprised.

"Are you still selling drugs for Harold?" asked Regina.

"Mind your own business; I'm going to take care of everything in here."

Missy and Curtis came out of the bedroom. Travis was not happy to see Curtis there.

"What's going on in here, Travis where have you been?" asked Missy. She was concerned.

"Who is this busta?" asked Travis.

"What's up, little man?" asked Curtis.

"I ain't your little man."

Curtis tried to shake Travis's hand.

"Man, get your punk ass out my face!"

"Curtis, just come back later sweetheart, I need to talk to my kids," said Missy.

"Yeah, sure baby. I will call you later." He left.

"Look, you little piece of shit, if you weren't bringing money in here, I would throw your ass out on your head."

Missy slammed him against the wall. "You just like your no good ass daddy. Now give me my money."

"Here take it, I don't care. I'll get more. I hate you! I hate you!" Travis gave Missy the roll of money and walked out.

Three months passed. Everything was pretty much the same as it was before. Regina was outside on the steps reading a book. A young man she had never seen before walked up.

"Hello, can I help you?" asked Regina.

"Hello, my name is John Anthony. I'm looking for Travis James."

"What do you want with Travis?" asked Regina.

"I'm trying to locate his family," said John Anthony.

"Is something wrong? I'm his sister Regina; we haven't seen him in months." She was very concerned.

"Oh, nothing like that. Travis has been staying at my grandmother's house with my little brother and I just wanted to find his folks," said John Anthony.

Regina sighed. "You scared me; I thought someone was looking for him to hurt him."

"Why would someone want to hurt Travis?" asked John Anthony.

"Because he sells drugs."

He was surprised. "Travis selling drugs, why would you think that?"

"He had a pocket full of money and was always coming home late," said Regina.

"Okay, I get it. You don't have to worry. Travis is not a drug dealer," said John Anthony.

"He's not?"

"No, he works for my cousin Harold at the race-track. Travis and my little brother Michael help Harold work on the race cars. Travis is very good at it. He can rebuild an engine all by himself. Harold says he has never seen anything like it," said John Anthony.

"I didn't know Travis liked cars."

"He's a good kid, smart mouth sometimes."

"Yeah, that's Travis."

"Can I come in and talk to your mother?" asked John.

"She's not here, just me. I'll tell her where Travis is staying."

"Have her give me a call. Let me give you my card," he said.

She looked at the card. "You work for the state. Is my mom in trouble?"

"Oh no, this is not an official visit or anything like that. I know your brother and I'm just trying to help him. I just moved back home a few months ago from Texas," said John Anthony.

"Texas, what were you doing out there."

"Well, I was in the military for four years."

"What made you want to come back here?" asked Regina.

"To help other young people like you."

"To help them do what?"

"Follow your dreams and get out of this hellhole. What do you like to do, Regina?" asked John.

"I like to read."

"That's great, do you want to go to college?"

"No, my mom says education won't get you out of here."

"So, your mother has a college degree?"

"No, she has lived here all her life. No one gets out."

"That's not true Regina. Your mother sounds programmed. Of course we can get out. I have a degree; I earned my degree while serving in the military. Give me a call and we can talk about it."

A year passed. Regina, with help from John Anthony, enlisted in the military after graduating from high school with honors.

Missy told Regina how proud she was of her. Missy asked Regina how the military life insurance works and whether she will be the beneficiary. The state gave Regina's sister Jasmine her kids back. She has been working two jobs taking care of them and has been drug free for over two years.

One day, Jasmine and Regina met. Regina was about to leave for her military training.

"Congratulations, booger rat," said Jasmine.

"Jasmine, don't call me booger rat."

"Okay, I'll stop. The girls made you a going away card," said Jasmine.

"They're beautiful. Tell them thank you and I will send them something once I'm finished with all of my training."

"Where is your training?"

"Ft. Jackson, South Carolina. Hey, here comes Travis."

"Hey, my beautiful sisters," said Travis.

Jasmine smiled. "He must need something."

"Yeah right! Congratulations, Regina. You are finally getting out of here. Are you happy?" asked Travis.

"Yes, but I am going to miss all of you guys," said Jasmine.

"Don't look back."

"I can't do that, you guys are my family."

"Yeah Travis, she always can come back home," said Jasmine.

"Whatever, I just wanted to come by and see you before you leave," said Travis.

"Are you going in to see Mama?"

"Hell no, I have nothing to say to her. You take care of yourself and keep in touch, love you. Jasmine, tell the girls Uncle Travis will see them this weekend."

Regina left for military training. The only one that didn't see her off was her sister Mary. Mary was never able to get off the drugs. Regina finished her training and was stationed at Ft. Lee, outside of Richmond, Virginia. After three years, Regina made the rank of Sergeant and went home for the Christmas holiday.

Missy was glad to see her. "Hey baby, I am so glad you're home. I made all your favorite foods. Put your bags in my room. You'll sleep in there just as you did last time you were home. You all move out the way and let Regina get by."

"I'm not staying here, Mama, I already have a hotel," said Regina.

"My baby is not staying at a hotel! What's wrong?"

"Nothing is wrong, Mama. I'd just rather stay at a hotel."

"Okay, I have some great news. Travis and I have been talking again after all these years. He is coming by for dinner."

"That's great Mom. How about Mary, have you heard from her?"

"No, your uncle George seen her a month ago downtown near some big crack house or something, I'm not sure."

"It's not easy; I've been there. I haven't seen her and I don't go around those places anymore," said Jasmine.

"Well, my friend Milton will be here in a few minutes."

"Mama, why do you continue to bring all these strange men around? It's not safe. You did the same thing when we were growing up and now Latoya has to see it."

"Mama needs a friend every now and then too, baby."

"I am going to take Latoya with me."

"Well, are you going to continue to send a check every month?" asked Missy.

Regina shook her head. "Is that all you care about!"

"Regina, don't worry about it. She will never change," said Jasmine.

Suddenly, Jasmine passed out and fell to the floor just as Travis walked in the door.

"What is going on, what happened?"

"Travis come quick! Mama, get some water. Girls, go in the other room."

Jasmine had become ill over the last couple of years and finally lost her battle with the sickle cell anemia disease. She passed away a few days after her fall. Regina not only took her little sister Latoya with her, but also Jasmine's two little girls. Regina retired from the military. Along with her husband, John Anthony Wright, they raised those three girls. They moved back to their home state and Regina ran for Congress. Now Representative Regina Wright was making a difference and helping people follow their dreams. Travis had his own race team and competed on the NASCAR circuit. Missy was still living in that two-bedroom apartment alone, and their sister Mary never came back home.

When seeing is believing, those who program what we see can influence what we believe.

THE END

WRITTEN BY RICHARD DENNIS MAYS

LOVE EVERLASTING

David Fogle and Terry Snipes were having lunch in downtown Austin. Both of them were very well dressed. The restaurant was filled with people. Everyone was busy with each other, eating, talking, and smiles all around.

Terry was busy with his phone.

"What are you doing, Terry?" asked David.

Terry looked at him. "I'm checking my Facebook page, Instagram, Twitter, and my Snapchat account."

"Man, if you spent as much time working as you spend on that social media crap, you would be a millionaire."

Terry smiled. "Stop, Hater. Look, I found several of my old high school friends on Facebook, man."

"Oh."

"Hey, you probably could hook up with some of your old girl friends from back in the day, playboy."

David was surprised. "Man, I don't want those kinds of problems. I went through a divorce and now a separation, about to get my second divorce, Man, you know that," said David.

"What does that have to do with anything? You're just re-connecting with old friends."

"I don't know, Terry, plus I don't know anything about social media."

"I can show you right quick, Man, it's easy."

Terry showed David how to sign up on Facebook.

Later, David was at home in his bedroom. He was on his new Facebook page scrolling through his friends list, and he got a message. He had thought very much about it as soon as Terry had told him about social media. And David had also found it amazing.

"Who is this messaging me, saying hello with the waving sign?" He looked at the picture.

"I think I recognize the picture; it looks like Tammy Sims, but it can't be." He shook his head.

"Naw, I haven't seen her since she was in high school, plus this name is Tammy Smith."

He was confused, but then he just decided to ask.

He typed a reply. "Hello there."

Almost simultaneously, he got an answer from the other end.

"Hi, long time no hear. How are you?"

"I'm fine. Not sure who this is?"

"Tammy Sims, now Smith. We use to date. Correction, we went to the same high school," said Tammy.

Now David was fully sure. "Girl I haven't seen you in forever. I have been asking about you for so long back home. How are you?" He was very excited.

"Yes, it has been a long time. I'm fine," said Tammy.

"That's good, it's good to hear from you."

"You live in Las Vegas now?"

"Yeah, I have been here since 2010."

"I lived in Dallas since 2014 for work."

"Did you like it?" asked David.

"Yes. Are you married?"

"Divorced, twice."

"I'm divorced also, only once for me. Not sure if I would get married again."

"I understand that, lol. Hey, if you wanted to talk outside of Facebook, give me a call some time and we can catch up. Here's my phone number," said David.

"Actually I already have it, did you know everyone can see your phone number on Facebook?"

David was confused. "No. I have no idea what I'm doing. This is my first time on social media."

Tammy sent laughing emojis. "I see. Here is my number as well."

Later the next day, David called Tammy. She was waiting for his call.

"Hey, it's David."

"Well hello there, it's good to hear your voice."

"Good to hear yours as well." He was laughing.

"Why are you laughing?" And she also laughed a bit.

"Because you sound the same after all these years."

"So do you! It's been a long time. I never thought I would hear your voice again. How long has it been?"

He thinks a bit. "About 30 years since we last saw each other," said David.

"That's a long time. Did we have sex the last time we saw each other?"

Again he laughed. "What? You don't remember? It must not have been that great if you don't remember."

"Actually I do. At the time, I also thought I may have been pregnant."

David was shocked to hear that. "Pregnant? Were you going to tell me if you were?"

"No, or maybe once I had it. Plus, I wasn't sure how to contact you, I knew you was in the military, but I would not want to make you feel you had to take care of my baby," said Tammy.

"I would have never let that happen; you should have known me better than that. Did I seem like someone that wouldn't take care of my responsibilities?"

"No, but if I had to do it alone, I would have."

"Plus you were on your way to college."

"Yes, and my sister was the one who encouraged me to go to college. She said she would help me with the baby, so I could continue to go to school, because that was so important as well."

"That would never have happened, I would have been by your side. But having a child would have changed both our lives. We would have gotten married and our paths would have changed."

"Married. I don't know about that. If so, I still would have finished school. I think we would have been okay."

"I remember like it was yesterday. We were driving around. I wasn't sure where we could go, then I remembered my parents were out of town, but my grandfather was at the house."

"Yes, I remember. I have to admit, you were my first and I had planned to have sex with you that night. I thought we would have a long relationship, but my plan was an epic failure. You didn't feel the same way about me as I felt about you."

"I don't think it was an epic failure. I did have strong feelings for you as well, I was in love, but I didn't express myself like I should have. I always thought about you over the years. Plus, when you went to college out of state, I didn't have a way to contact you."

"I gave you my sister's phone number," Tammy reminded him.

"You did. I am so sorry. I must have lost it. Now that you say that, I do remember you giving me her information. I am so sorry. Every time I came home on leave from the military, I asked if anyone had heard anything from you, but no one had."

"I never came home much at all. I wanted to stay as far away from there as possible. Very bad memories with my family, long story," said Tammy.

"Yes, I remember some things that were going on. We all have family problems from back then. It was hard growing up in that small town. I am so proud of you for the woman you have become. Very successful and still very beautiful."

"Thank you; you don't look so bad yourself, still handsome. Those pictures you sent me, wow; you are still in shape as well."

"You're going to get yourself in trouble talking like that."

"Why not, we both grownups, right?"

"Yes, we are."

They both smiled.

David and Tammy talked for hours every night, sometimes until they both fell asleep on the phone like teenagers. They had fallen in love all over again.

Three months later, Tammy was calling David. Finally, he picked up.

"Hey baby," said Tammy.

"Hello gorgeous, are we still meeting up back home next week?"

"Yes, but I'm a little nervous about meeting your mother for the first time. You never told her we had sex in her house back in the day, did you?"

"No, that was a long time ago. My mother and I are cool, she wouldn't think anything about that now anyway."

"Do not tell her that."

David laughed.

"Some of your old girlfriends are going to be pretty upset when they see us together."

"No, you don't have to worry about anything like that. But I do have something to tell you," said David.

"What's that?"

"When we first reconnected months ago, my divorce paperwork was in the courts for the sixty-day waiting period. Because of the Coronavirus, everything was put on hold."

Tammy got a bit upset. "So what does that mean?"

"I am not sure. I think since the waiting period has passed, all I have to do is sign the paperwork. If not, we may have to file the paperwork again," David said.

"So you are still married?"

"Yes technically, but we've been separated for over a year."

"No, for us to continue, you have to be divorced. I do not have relationships with married men, I never have, and I never will."

David was surprised. He tried to convince her. "I promise. Baby. I will fix this."

"Well, until you do. I feel that we should just be friends."

"What? Come on, Tammy, don't do this, it's not a big deal," said David.

"Not a big deal? You are a married man. We can't start a relationship like that."

"I didn't mean for it to sound like that."

"How do I know you are not going back to your wife," Tammy said.

"Oh no, we are over. Look Tammy, we have this rare opportunity to be reconnected after all these years. Please let's not throw this away. Let me fix this."

"Like I said, until you fix it, we should just be friends."

"I understand, I will. Are we still getting a room together when we meet up? I have a lot of plans."

"I hope it's not involving sex, because I am not having sex with a married man."

"Oh, I understand that, but other things. You know, so you can relax after your long trip."

"David, I don't want to do anything that may lead to sex. It's been a very long time for me, and I don't want any temptations."

"Not even a hot bubble bath, apple martini, and my special massage?"

"No! Tempting."

"Nothing?"

"Nothing."

Later, David called his wife and fortunately for him the time period had passed. They signed the paperwork, and the divorce was final. Two weeks after the divorce, David and Tammy met in a downtown hotel.

Both of them were very happy as it was the right moment and everything turned out as they had thought. Finally, they were together again.

"I am so happy everything worked out."

Tammy, with a broader smile on her face, replied, "So am I."

"I can't remember a time I have been so happy. Being here with you makes me whole again. I feel that God has given me a second chance at life. But I have to be honest about something." David looked a little sad.

With a caring expression, Tammy asked, "What's that, baby?"

David sighed and looked down, then replied, "I have this guilty feeling in the pit of my stomach about my ex-wife. Don't get me wrong, it's not a loving feeling."

"David, I understand. I know exactly what you're feeling."

David was silent.

"I was married for over twenty years and probably should have left after the first five years. I didn't because of the same thing. The fear of making the other person suffer. The unhealthy and unjustified feeling that we are the ones responsible for their well-being leads us to stay in the relationship that isn't working, or we never leave at all. I read that it leads us to a state of constant standby, in which we don't follow through with what we want to do out of fear of making the other person suffer. That's how time passes. That's how your life can pass you by," said Tammy.

"The one who leaves can't carry the other person's pain."

Tammy smiled and says, "That's right. You will be fine; we will be fine."

David and Tammy went on to get married. They spent the rest of their days making each other happy. Who says you can't go back again?

THE END

STORY NO. 10:

WRITTEN BY RICHARD DENNIS

MAYS AND GARY STHEPHENS

I NEED A HUG

It was a bright, sunny morning. There was a large house on the corner of the street. It belonged to Christopher and Melissa Mann.

Christopher Mann was humming a song in the shower; he got out and headed back into the bedroom to get something. Melissa had just left the bedroom and walked downstairs, leaving her laptop open on the bed.

Christopher glanced at the screen. "What is this, a dating site?"

He looked more carefully at it. "What the hell. Who the heck is Derek?"

Melissa was coming back upstairs. "Hey babe, are you still in the shower?"

He ran back in the bathroom. "No, I'm shaving. What's up?"

"Just wondering."

"Okay."

"Are you going to be able to drop the kids off to school?" asked Melissa.

"I drop them off every day. Why would today be any different?"

"Don't start, Cris. You know I can't drop the kids off; I have to be at work earlier than you, you know that. That was one of the stipulations we made when I transferred here to Charlotte from LA."

Christopher started getting dressed. "Stipulation you made. I never agreed to that."

"So now you're going to pout about it?"

"Pouting? Listen."

Suddenly, their son, Ahmad, walked in. "Dad, where are my clothes for school?" asked Ahmad.

"After I washed them, I didn't have time to put them away. Look in the laundry room in the blue basket," said Christopher.

"Look, I have to fly out this morning."

He was surprised. "I thought you didn't have to fly out until Monday. Why would you have to leave now?"

"My mom and sisters are getting together for a mother-daughter night."

"What about your daughter?" asked Christopher.

"I will do something with the kids when I get back." She put her suitcase on the bed.

"You can't keep buying their love, Melissa. They want your time, not gifts."

Then he noticed something. "What's that?" Something was hanging out of the suitcase.

"What?"

"Is that lingerie?"

She got nervous. "Just something nice I picked up from Victoria's Secret, my sister has something like this."

"You don't wear lingerie for me, but you're going to wear it for your sister," said Christopher.

"No, silly. I saw hers, and I just wanted to get something nice. I bought it on my last trip, no big deal."

He got more curious. "No big deal? We haven't had sex in six months."

"You haven't said anything. Look, I have to get to work. We can talk about this later."

Before he could say anything, she left.

Christopher made the kids breakfast and took them to school. Later that evening, once Christopher got the kids settled, he called his best friend, Jefferson Bailey.

"Jeff, what up, boy."

"What up, Cris, man, you are going to live a long time. My mom and I were talking about you. She says you are this close to South Carolina and never come home. She hasn't seen you in years, my brother."

"I know, man, tell Ms. Ella I am sorry, and she will be the first one I see when I come home next month," said Christopher.

"I will, man, you know how it is. They're getting old, man, we all are. What's going on, man, you good?"

"Same old stuff, man, nothing has changed," said Christopher.

"You and Melissa still having issues?"

"Yeah, but it's not just that. I feel like nothing is going right in my life, sometimes. I don't even feel like doing anything with the kids. I don't do any of the things we use to do when we were kids or when we were in the Navy together."

"You don't even play basketball anymore?"

"No man, don't have the desire. It seems like no one cares. Like the entire world is against me."

"Hey, brother, I care. Hey, you know, my baby sister Nicole lives in Charlotte as well. I was planning on visiting her anyway. It's only two and a half hours away. I'll be there tonight. I'll let you know when I get there."

"Jeff, man, you don't have to do that. I'll be fine."

"You were there for me brother, when I was going through my divorce and my custody battle. Of course I am going to be there for you. I'll call you when I get to Nicole's house."

Later that night, Jefferson was at his sister's house. He decided to text Christopher.

"Hey Cris, I am at my sister's house. I'll text you the address. She wants you to come to dinner tomorrow. Bring the kids; her girls will be here."

And he got a reply from the other end. "Cool, man, text me the address and time she wants us to be there."

"OK, man. Are you good, you need to talk?"

"No, bro, I am good. I'll see you guys tomorrow."

Next day in the afternoon, Christopher and his kids reached the house of Jefferson's sister. He pressed the doorbell. The door opened; it was Nicole, Jefferson's sister.

"Hey there, how are you doing, Cris?"

They hug.

"I haven't seen you kids since you were little. Come on in, everybody's in the dining room."

They walked in.

"Let me introduce you to my family. This is my husband, Melvin, and my daughters, Mya and Lisa. This is Melvin's mother, Ms. Liz, and you know Jefferson, of course."

"Hello, everyone, and these are my kids. Willow and Ahmad, say hello, guys," said Christopher.

"Hello."

"Welcome. Jeff tells me you guys were in the Navy together."

Christopher nodded and replied, "Yeah, Norfolk, Virginia."

"Melvin was in the Army. But we want to hold that against him."

"Yeah yeah yeah, you got jokes," said Melvin.

"What was your MOS? My dad was in the Army," said Christopher.

"I was a Calvary Scout," said Melvin.

"Scout's out!"

"What you know about Scout's out?"

"My father was a Scout. He changed his MOS after his first enlistment, but he always talks about his time in the Scouts."

"Once a Scout, always a Scout."

"Did you like it?" asked Christopher.

"Not all the time, but it was the best decision I ever made, other than marrying this beautiful woman."

Nicole looked at him and smiled. "Oh, thank you, baby." She kissed him on his cheek.

Later, after everyone ate, Jefferson and Christopher got to talk in the living room.

"Hey Cris, let's go in the living room, man. The kids will be fine, my nieces will take care of them," said Jefferson.

"Oh, I know that, bro," said Christopher.

"You want something to drink? Melvin and my sister have a full bar."

"No, man, I seldom drink anymore," said Christopher.

"Yeah, that's probably for the best if you're feeling depressed, brother. Hey, I was going to ask you. Have you been using your VA benefits?" asked Jefferson.

"No?"

"They have programs for veterans. I'll text you the number, and you can call them and make an appointment. They also have a crisis line."

"Thanks, brother, I will check it out. Yeah, that's not all, a few months ago I had meningitis."

"Meningitis? Man, I don't know a lot about meningitis."

"Man, it was awful."

Jefferson was shocked.

"Meningitis is a rare infection that causes inflammation of the meninges, which are the membranes that surround the brain and spinal cord. Man, this disease can be caused by bacterial or viral infections, or from fungal or parasitic infections as well. It depends on how serious the condition is. Most of the time, it can be treated by medication, but it can also be fatal."

"My God, man, why didn't you tell me, bro? How are you doing now, you need anything?"

Christopher was trying to look normal. "No, bro, I am better, but I can't hear as well out of my right ear and I've had some memory loss."

"Man, I am so sorry. What did Melissa say?"

"Not much of anything."

Again Jefferson was surprised. "What!"

"She didn't seem that concerned, I mean not like I felt she should have been. And I told her I was suffering from anxiety and depression."

"And what did she say?"

Christopher shook his head. "She told me to man up and get over it."

Jefferson could not believe it. "No, you have got to be kidding?"

"No."

"Does she know anything about mental health?" asked Jefferson.

"No, she does not, apparently."

Jefferson was in complete shock to hear all that. "Unbelievable…"

Unfortunately, one month later, Christopher committed suicide. Jefferson spoke at the funeral about Christopher's struggles with anxiety and depression and the importance of knowing the signs. And to make sure you get people the help they need.

THE END

AUTHOR BIOGRAPHY

Richard Dennis Mays is an American entrepreneur, the co-founder and co-CEO of Shared Wysdom, LLC. Richard is a short filmmaker, writer, actor, director, producer, and author of his debut book, Amazing Short Stories for Grown-Ups. He is a retired military veteran who served 22 years in the U.S. Army. Richard has a business degree from American Intercontinental University, and he studied drama at Central Texas College. He also studied film at the Austin School of Film in Austin, Texas. `Richard's mission is to motivate, uplift, inspire, and encourage others to exceed their own dreams and expectations.

9 781649 904867